Dissenting Opinion from the Committee for the Beatitudes

Dissenting Opinion from the Committee for the Beatitudes

Marc J. Sheehan

Etchings Press
Indianapolis, Indiana
2019

This publication is made possible by funding provided by the College of Arts and Sciences and the English Department at the University of Indianapolis. Special Thanks to IngramSpark and to the students who judged, designed, and edited this chapbook: Tayah Eakle, Larson Hicks, and Bryson Hile.

UNIVERSITY *of*
INDIANAPOLIS.

Published by Etchings Press
1400 E. Hanna Ave.
Indianapolis, Indiana, 46227
All rights reserved

etchings.uindy.edu
www.uindy.edu/cas/english

Printed by IngramSpark
ingramspark.com

Published in the United States of America

ISBN 978-0-998897-6-2-2
23 22 21 20 19   1 2 3 4 5

Table of Contents

The Biennese

Jill and I were unloading the car, schlepping our backpacks and bags of groceries into the cabin, when Sonny stopped his pick-up to check us out. He lived in the woods full-time, owned an incongruous brick ranch house at the very end of the two-track that meandered like a river of sand past working-class vacation shacks and hunting camps.

I hadn't been at my family's place in a while, and he didn't recognize me at first—me with my long hair and beard—who was getting away from the city for a weekend with my girlfriend.

"Sorry," he said, still sitting in the cab of the idling truck. "We've had a bunch of B&E's around here. I just wanted to make sure you belong."

I was lying in bed that night, feeling the length of Jill's skin and listening languidly to the silence when she asked me if all the people around here were that racist.

"What do you mean?" I asked.

"The Biennese. That guy said he wanted to make sure we weren't Biennese," she said.

I explained that he was talking about Breaking and En-tering.

"Oh," Jill said, rolling onto me. "And how do you know so much about crime? Who are you, anyway?"

Her long brown hair rained down as she lowered herself to kiss me.

"I'm your little Biennese, baby," I whispered in her ear.

If your guess is that I managed to screw things up, you're right. Sometimes I go online and visit the website Jill launched to sell her art. I look at photos of her at various gallery openings and wish I had been there over the years to witness the arrival of each wrinkle and gray hair. It's sort of like being a Peeping Tom, which is exactly what you'd expect of a Biennese.

Recently I dreamed I was in an automat, but instead of sandwiches and soft drinks displayed behind little windows, the machines vended other lives. I could see them there behind the glass—or maybe they were video screens. In each tiny diorama Jill was next to me, no larger than a figure atop a wedding cake. I reached into my pocket for some coins, but they were from another country.

The Dauphin

President Agnew is tired after his daily briefing and ready to watch a re-run of *The Love Boat*. Next to his glass of jug wine on the kitchen table rests The Football, an old scuffed Detroit Lions model. He refuses to go anywhere without it. He often complains about the responsibility of knowing the nuclear codes.

It's a mystery how, when my father's dementia struck, it took the form of his belief that he is President Spiro T. Agnew. Father was never political. He did get upset when Gerald Ford, the representative of our west Michigan district, became president without being elected, but not enough to even write a letter to the *Grand Rapids Press*.

Now it's 1984, after what would have been the Agnew administration, and long after I gave up athletics for chasing girls and smoking pot. Back in junior high I was a second-string quarterback and Dad, already in his fifties, used to jog across the yard with his arms outstretched for a catch as I practiced my spiral.

In the spring when I got laid off from my office job, I moved back in to spend time with him and give Mom a rest. The wine and *Love Boat* is everyone's reward for getting through another afternoon cabinet meeting.

"Are we doing all we can to further relations with China?" he asks. "After everything that's happened to Dick, I think it's the least we can do."

"Yes, Mr. President," I say, "although Chairman Mao is unpredictable as always."

"Would the president like Salisbury steak or turkey and peas for dinner?" asks my mother, the Secretary of the Interior.

President Agnew ponders, a finger stroking the pebbly surface of the football. "Turkey and peas," he announces.

"Then the Vice President is having Salisbury steak," she says, looking at me. "The White House kitchen has only one turkey and peas."

We've had frozen dinners most nights since an x-ray found a tumor, inoperable and fast-growing, in the president's lung. The doctor said we could try radiation and chemo but thought the cure would kill him faster than the disease. Before the x-ray we had gently tried to convince him he is not President Agnew.

Summer drags on. We survive the Mayaguez Incident, the Fall of Saigon, and Hoffa's disappearance. His breath becomes shallow and labored, even with the flow from the oxygen tank cranked up high. By mid-September it's just mother and me sitting at the kitchen table, drinking rosé and watching ocean-borne romance with the sound turned low while the president drowses in his recliner.

One night after eating our microwave dinners on TV trays in the living room, I help get the president dressed in his pajamas and tucked into bed. I ask him if he wants to keep up with events. He nods and I turn on the portable Magnavox perched on my parents' dresser. Father cradles the football next to him atop the chenille bedspread. He has the little nozzle portion of the plastic tubing from the green tank in his nose. The oxygen makes a hissing sound as he stares blankly at a man shaving his thickly foamed face with a disposable razor.

"You'll make sure everything is okay when I'm gone, won't you?" he wheezes. I don't know who's asking me this—my father, or Spiro Agnew.

"Yes, I will, Mr. President. Dad," I say. He smiles. Then

he nudges the football up onto his stomach where he can
grab it firmly and hands it off to me.

The Museum of Tears

My wife and I are standing in the lobby of a motel
perusing the usual rack of tourist attraction brochures. I like
motels. They make me feel as if I'm on the lam, although I
am not a very lam-prone person.

Where ya wanna go before we pull us our next bank job,
I ask, doing my best Clyde Barrow impersonation. Bonnie,
let's call her, picks up a brochure for the Museum of Tears
and says she wants to go there.

Or, I say, we could go to the Museum of Fashion Design
and pretend to be mannequins.

We have vials of tears from Mother Teresa, Jerry Lewis,
and Richard Nixon, Bonnie reads out loud.

Or we could go to the Rock & Roll Hall of Fame and
feel bad about not being famous, I warble.

The Museum of Tears has a Dylan impersonator who
sings "Tears of Rage" on the half-hour, Bonnie mumbles.

Or we could go to the Museum of Natural History, I say
in my indoor voice, and reaffirm our belief in evolution.

I want to ask forgiveness at the shrine of Avalokitesh-
vara, the Bodhisattva of Infinite Compassion, who created
his consort, Tara, by shedding a single tear, Bonnie says
reverently.

Or we could go to the Museum of Bad Art and look at
examples of derivative, paint-by-numbers Surrealism, I float
as a trial balloon shaped like a green apple.

But, Bonnie declares with some passion, the Museum of
Tears has free parking.

Or we could visit the Museum of Useless Things and
buy many commemorative Useless Things from their gift
shop, I reply uselessly.

Marc J. Sheehan || 7

Museum of Tears! Museum of Tears! Bonnie cries.
So that's where we go.

What I'd Say to Aliens

For years the doll sat on a small rocking chair in the guest bedroom. People often have guest bedrooms even if they seldom have guests. The doll was slightly less than half my height when held up so that its feet just touched the floor. It wore a yellow sundress with a pattern that consisted of small red flowers alternating with tiny blue hearts and had a kind of shoe called Mary Janes. The shoes were red and made out of felt. Its features—slightly parted lips, mole on its right cheek, hair that fell over its forehead in dark bangs—consisted, like the Mary Janes, of felt. The resemblance to me was uncanny.

A friend of mine made it as a present for my wedding. There had been a mate, which I doubt exists any longer, although the man it had been based on still does. I guess. The doll had a snap in the middle of its left hand which originally allowed it to be joined to the husband doll. Do you know what a stigmata is? It was like that except silver, and bloodless, and sewn to a hand that had just four fingers.

The doll did little to distinguish itself from a menagerie of stuffed animals spread across the guest bed and atop an antique dresser. Many times during those years I thought I should re-read that essay about dolls by this writer named Rilke. Although I cleaned the doll many times with a Dust Buster, I never managed to go back to Rilke.

When my cat died I decided to finally have new carpeting installed, promising myself I would not give in to sentimentality and get another pet. People often do that. Ladysmith Blue Petunia's absence combined with having to clean out closets for the installation triggered in me a desire to finally get rid of things. I carted off outmoded computers to the recycling center and left various side tables and lamps by the curbside, looking out the window every few minutes to see how long it would take before someone stopped to pick them up. I was pretty sure they would, and they did.

After I had crammed most of the stuffed animals into a cardboard box, I picked up the doll. Its arms and legs ended up in unnatural angles when I put it in a black plastic trash bag. That can happen.

I drove boxes of books, an old stereo and armloads of clothes that no longer fit to the Goodwill, but I left the doll on the floor in back just behind the driver's seat. I thought I would wait for a few days to get rid of it, to make sure that I really wanted it out of my life. Sometimes people can regret hasty decisions. I have a long commute and my car is usually a jungle of fast-food containers, unread reports and extra shoes—none of which are Mary Janes—so one more bag wasn't going to make much of a difference.

When the doll still sat on the floor of the backseat a month later, I hardly even noticed it any longer. That, too, can happen. The trash bag blended in well with the car's dark interior and with the black laptop computer case I haul back and forth to work each day. One rainy morning in the employee parking lot I grabbed a rumpled overcoat that had been lying on the backseat for weeks. When I pulled the coat out it caught on the trash bag and pulled it open enough to expose the doll.

That essay by Rilke has to do with dolls calling out to us to give life to them. Or maybe I think that only because the doll looked so dead. Memory is like that—it's a storyteller, not an accountant like me. The doll was doubled over the way I imagine an actual body might to make it fit.

There are stories in which dolls really do come to life. I

wasn't afraid of that happening. This ain't *The Twilight Zone* or *Bride of Chucky* or even *Pinocchio*. When your worst fear is to start crying in the rain in front of fellow employees hurrying to get to a warm cubicle, that is horror by other means.

So when you see a woman take her doppelgänger which, once upon a time, celebrated a union unto death and toss it, with feigned calm, into a dumpster, trust me, do not fuck with her.

Your powers are useless.

Divorce Party

Friends gave us towels with "Not His" and "Not Hers" written in rough, glittery epoxy, mismatched wine glasses, and CDs in the wrong jewel cases. Eric, a mail-order minister, oversaw our anti-vows and we exchanged plastic gumball machine rings.

A year later my ex took a job out of state—a move I blessed out of stupidity and a misunderstanding of the Buddhist tenant of nonattachment.

Sometimes, when the hamper is full and the Laundromat too awful to contemplate, I use the "Not Hers" towel, whose words are so rough they leave long, unromantic scratches if I forget to avoid them.

The Origins of Omniscient Man

Tim, Kent, Sid, and I are hanging out at Sid's place debating, yet again, the perfect ratio of gin to vermouth. Every month the four of us get together for a martini party since we live within walking distance of each other and so don't have to argue over who will be the designated driver. Our ex-wives and ex-girlfriends all graduated from the doctoral psychology program at the local university, and we have stayed in touch after each break-up and divorce.

During the second pitcher of martinis, Kent asks which superpower we'd choose if we could have one. Tim is for super-human strength and Kent decides upon invisibility. I say I want to be omniscient—at least then I could get a teaching job with tenure. Tim points out that if I knew everything, it wouldn't matter what department had an opening, either.

Sid says he wants the ability to summon lost things back to him.

"Whaddya mean?" Kent asks.

"When I was a kid my parents got divorced, so there was always a toy or something I wanted that was at my other parent's house, and lots of stuff got lost or thrown out. I wanted to make the thing appear by just thinking about it," Sid says.

Feeling relaxed from the gin, I flip through Sid's collection of vinyl LPs trying to find something to put on the stereo since it's my turn to choose. He buys a lot of off-beat records at second-hand stores, and I want to spin something suitably ironic. "Would it just, like, materialize?" I ask.

"No. The thing would sort of fly through the air," he says. "Sometimes I'd keep my window open at night so my bottle cap collection could land on my bed."

I put an album of steel-drum music on the turntable.

The record label is decorated with a colorful map of Trinidad—the spindle rising from the country's interior highland. There's Trinidad, but no Tobago. Poor Tobago, I think.

"So, anything you lost you could get back," Tim says. "That's cool."

Sid kills his martini and starts making a third pitcher, splashing in extra gin—ratio be damned. "Actually, anything you've ever touched you could make come to you," he says. "I thought about writing a comic book featuring a hero with that power. He would have to resist stealing, because he could have anything he's ever been in contact with."

Kent says moral dilemmas are always good.

"I don't imagine the FAA would like it if you made a Mercedes fly to your driveway," I say. "Plus, you'd have to live in some place like the Fortress of Solitude so people wouldn't see all this stuff zipping across the sky to your house."

Tim uses a pickle fork to spear olives out of a jar and deliver them to our empty glasses. "Would your super-power apply to people? Could you make someone fly to you?" he asks.

"I guess so," Sid says, "I never thought about that."

"You'd need to be careful," I say. "If you got lonely and thought about your ex-wife you might make her crash through your front door."

Sid stirs the martinis and shrugs his shoulders. "Our marriage wasn't all bad. The first couple years were good," he says.

Kent holds out his glass. "That raises the question of whether the person would be the person he or she is now, or the person you remember," he says. "Say you thought about your ex-wife as she was the day you got married. Would she be that person, exactly as she was then?"

The extra gin Sid put in the pitcher fills our glasses up to their brims. I take a sip so I won't spill any on the coffee table, although it already has many stains from glasses and mugs. I am sitting on the floor where I have LP covers spread out around me, including the cover for the steel-drum band whose musicians wear nifty puffy-sleeved calypso outfits. "It would be like that Chagall painting," I say. "The one with the woman in the wedding dress who's floating above the house? Except I think there's also a goat and a violinist."

"We should start small with the super-powers," Tim suggests. "I say we go with one person or thing at a time."

So we move to the backyard to see if Sid can make his ex-wife appear.

It's late September, the weather mild. We sit in a line of mismatched lawn chairs staring into the darkness above Sid's rental, passing a steadily emptier bottle of gin back and forth to freshen our drinks. A few blocks over a red light atop a broadcasting tower blinks on and off, as do the lights of a jet. Steel-drum music pongs through the screen door, but when that ends it's quiet.

I wonder what it would feel like to be the person flying through the air because someone missed you that much. Maybe you'd believe you were being taken up in the rapture since some end-of-world prediction is always in the news, or else think scientists had finally screwed up gravity with one of their experiments. But then why are you wearing this frothy dress, this swallowtail coat, this swimsuit you looked good in just that one summer?

By now I've changed my mind. I don't want to be super-intelligent. Secretly, I want someone to grant me the ability to fly. We all do. I mean, nobody says that, but I know.

The Sad Decline of the Sideshow

The first thing I thought of when my boyfriend gave
his heart to me was this *shrunken* head my cousin bought at
some carnival one summer when we were kids. It had that
same creepy, wizened, you know, shrunken quality to it. The
heart *was* made of plastic and about the size of a strawber-
ry—organic, since that was the only kind he would eat. It
was painted with red hobbyist paint ("Mythical Maroon")
and its atriums, ventricles and other stuff you don't want to
know about were delineated by thin lines of black enamel my
boyfriend had painstakingly applied himself. It looked like
an artifact from an alien autopsy, or proof that the Grinch's
heart really *was* two sizes too small. He presented it to me
strung on a thin silver chain.

The summer my cousin, Steve, bought the shrunken
head, he was nine and I was seven. His mom, my dad's sister,
was a single mother and sometimes Steve stayed with us because his mom thought he needed a male role model. As any
nine-year-old boy would know, a shrunken head is the perfect
thing with which to frighten an unsuspecting younger cousin.
He got the chance to ambush me with it because instead of
going with him and Dad to the carnival, Mom took me to
see *Disney on Ice*.

The heart was an anatomically correct reproduction of
my boyfriend's own heart—a sort of scaled-down, model car
version. His father had died young of an infarction, so when
he experienced some tightness in his chest his doctor ordered
an MRI. The pain went away, and everything looked nor-
mal. When the doctor showed him the images on the computer, my boyfriend thought they were cool and talked the
physician into giving them to him on a flash drive. He's good

at talking people into doing stuff. It's one of the many things he's proud of.

The first thing I saw the morning I woke up after seeing *Disney on Ice* was the shrunken head. I screamed, which was extraordinarily gratifying to my cousin, who stood at the foot of my bed dangling the head in front of my face by means of my father's seldom-used fishing pole. He reeled the head in and took off down the hall in his pajamas before my parents stumbled in, groggy, to see what was wrong.

There were enough MRI images from different angles that my boyfriend was able to blend them together into one digital 3-D file on his computer. Then he took the file to a rapid prototyping shop and had them print out the heart. Our relationship was not going well, and this was his attempt at being capital-R Romantic—something I may have told him was not his forte. Although I knew it wouldn't help, I clasped the silver chain on around my neck. And although I knew it, too, wouldn't help, I made love with him that night. His heart kept hitting me on my chest.

The head had straggly black hair, and stitches to keep its mouth and eyes closed. Steve developed a long story about the head—how a missionary went to Java and brought it back after living with a remote tribe. The missionary lost his faith during his years in the jungle, and eventually became a cannibal and head-hunter himself. The story included a long description of what it took to shrink a head, which involved removing the brains and burying the head in burning sand.

My cousin and I came to a kind of truce that summer. I remember a tea party I held with my dolls. We invited the shrunken head who came and behaved really very civilly. He had, after all, a certain charisma, a mythic depth of character. The heart, on the other hand, wasn't really a heart.

A heart is shaped like a valentine, or the symbol on an I ♥
NY t-shirt. A heart does more than just pump blood. You
can be of two minds about something, but not two hearts.
I wasn't looking for a shrunken aorta, but a dagger-pierced,
Cupid-arrowed, sugary-diabetic-coma-inducing, burning-
through-the-chest-of-Jesus, carved-into-birch-bark-with-
our-names-and-a-plus-sign-equalling-forever heart. A heart
bigger than a heart—that's the only kind worth capturing.
Everyone knows this: hermaphrodites, four-legged women,
fire-breathers, human blockheads, mermaids, sword-swal-
lowers, tattooed women, dog-faced boys, Siamese twins, even
Tom Thumb, the world's shortest man, whose heart was
the size of a blue-ribbon berry and whose head looked only
slightly too big.

The Umamist

First of all, what *is* Umami? It is the fifth taste beyond sweet, sour, salty and bitter. Like the sixth sense, there are people who don't believe it exists. Like intuition, it is subtler, less quantifiable. My step-father, an electrician, said that once, during the Depression, his boss was hiring a new crew and treated the candidates to lunch at Walgreens. He hired the men who did not salt their food before tasting it. Those men would make sure the current was turned off before touching a wire. That's Umami. Umami is not your first kiss, but your second. It's a character's motivation, the back story. Umami is less taste-bud than Rosebud. As a young man my grandfather, who spent his life working in a lumberyard, was recruited by the Chicago Cubs, but his family wouldn't let him go to the big city. He could have been bitter, but he was Umami. It is the computer program running in the background, creating a trail of cookies. It's the bass player in a rock band, or perhaps the band's last original member, or both. Umami is the revelation you have at 2 a.m. but can't remember. Umami is singing karaoke when you're sober. It is badly translated assembly instructions and the left-over parts. Umami is taking this class to meet someone, or because you need an excuse to get out of the house. I see you're nodding. Very good, we are ready to cook now.

Paradoxes of the Space-Time Continuum

"It's like living just slightly in the future," Ed says. I used to hang out with him in high school, then didn't see him for years until my mother's funeral. He looks pretty much the same. His long curly hair is streaked with gray, but he seems otherwise nearly untouched by the passing years. The effect is doubly disconcerting seeing him here in this small town where we grew up.

"I saw a *Twilight Zone* episode once about this guy who steals a camera that takes pictures of what will happen in a few minutes," I say. "It didn't end well."

Like Ed, the local tavern also seems almost unchanged. Perhaps the stuffed muskrat next to the pickled bologna is a little more glassy-eyed, and the shuffleboard table is now seriously retro. For the past half-hour, Ed and I have been riffing on the metaphysics of bars having their own time zone twenty minutes in the future. And why not?

After the ham-sandwich-and-potato-salad gathering at the American Legion Hall ("fellowship," as the rented pastor put it), the mourners had slowly drifted away—surviving friends of my mother ferried by their aging sons and daughters. Now, all that's left for me to do is continue packing up my mother's house, readying it for sale. This is the perfect place to kill an afternoon, I think, in a sort of mental faux pas.

"Okay. You know when you drive past a pile of burning leaves?" Ed asks.

"They don't let you do that anymore," I point out. "Global warming." Ed nods his head solemnly over the injustice of it. The ban on burning, not the warming. "Anyway, back when you still *could* you'd drive past a pile of leaves and wouldn't smell it until you were down the road."

"Or, like, once I was hunting with my uncle who was on the other side of this field," I offer. "He shot a six-point and I saw it drop before I heard the shot."

"You never hear the one that gets you," Ed says. I drain the last of my beer before heading to the men's room.

"I need to use the facilities, or this beer I'm having in the future I'll be pissing in the past," I say.

When I return from the bathroom Ed is gone. On the bar there are a few crumpled bills next to our empty glasses. Assuming he's gone outside to smoke, I pour myself into my own jacket and push out into the cold March sunlight.

He's not there. I guess he didn't want me to talk him out of driving. I'm just going to stroll back to Mother's place, but he lives an hour away and came over for the funeral in the red, over-powered Trans Am he bought new more than thirty years ago and has maintained religiously ever since. It's a cop magnet.

I start walking. It takes just a few minutes to get to Mom's place, so I'll arrive around the time I left or, perhaps, am leaving. It's like on the various incarnations of *Star Trek* when characters get teleported from the starship Enterprise. It's a convenient plot twist to have someone beamed down to check out an alien world, then unable to get back. It's like after someone dies. There you are on a strange planet, stranded.

"Do you mean 'acts of contrition' or 'sins of omission'"?
I ask Paul, my seat-mate.

"I mean 'sins of contrition,'" he says.

We are somewhere over the Atlantic on our way from London to Boston. The detritus of the food service has been cleared away, and the in-flight movie has thankfully come to an end. The action flick's chase scenes along with turbulence combined to make my processed chicken dinner churn in my stomach. The flight is not crowded and most of the other passengers are drowsing beneath thin airline blankets or reading trashy novels in the glow of their over-head lights.

Paul has his own reading light on, which doesn't make the sunglasses he continues to wear any less pretentious. He is well dressed in some brand of gray, designer-label suit, the jacket of which is draped over the empty seat in front of him. The light is focused on his freshly pressed white shirt complete with gold cufflinks embossed with a coat of arms. He wears a pair of incongruous snakeskin boots. I have the aisle seat, he has the window. Between us on the tray of the unoccupied middle seat are several empty miniature bottles of brandy. We have the contents of the last two of them in our plastic glasses and Paul has his eye out to get us refills. He says he's a TV producer. I think he's bullshitting me, but he insists on paying for the drinks, so I'm cool with it. He flags down the flight attendant on her way to the galley. He waggles one of the empty bottles.

"Last call," she says, eyeing our empties.

"In that case, make it a double for both of us," Paul says. Once we settle back in with our drinks resting on the tray cleared of our empties he continues, "It's going to be a reality show."

"What is?" I ask.

"Sins of Contrition. It's about people who do bad things in order to do good," he explains. "It's sort of an 'ends justifies the means' kind of thing."

"Doing good isn't the same thing as being contrite," I say.

"True," he says, "but it's a catchy title. We'll have a line or two of voice-over at the beginning of each episode, or maybe a theme song, to explain the premise. For the pilot we've got a guy who embezzled money to pay for his wife's cancer treatment." It takes me a moment to understand that the pilot is the supposed first episode of the series, not the person in the cockpit.

It was just a month ago, although it seems like much longer, that the care facility my mother was living in called me before dawn one morning. She had started moaning and clutching her stomach. She had been slowly declining both mentally and physically for some time and the decline accelerated during her final months. She hadn't known who I was for a couple of years, and in her last weeks was barely able to talk. She had virtually given up eating. When the pain began, she was unable to say what the problem was and simply rocked from side to side in her bed. The facility helped arrange hospice care, which started that same day thanks to a couple of frantic phone calls I placed. Someone else might have rushed her to the hospital and insisted on x-rays and exploratory surgery, but she was 93-years-old and putting her through that seemed cruel.

What surprised me was the open secret that administering morphine for her pain would end her life. The caregivers

at the facility told me as much, and the hospice workers explained how the drug would slow down her body's functions
to the point where they "might not be sustainable."

She died the next night.

My mother's name was Elvis. Once the other Elvis got
popular, she had to keep a copy of her birth certificate in
her purse to be sure that cashiers would take her checks. She
claimed her name should have been Elvis Really, because
that's what everyone said the first time they met her. Late one
afternoon shortly before she died, I arrived to find her in the
facility's common area. She was sitting in her wheelchair being serenaded by an Elvis impersonator who was holding her
hand while softly singing "Love Me Tender," to her. It was
beautiful and awful. I walked quickly down the corridor to
her room to get some Kleenex and compose myself. When I
came back the faux Elvis in his white jumpsuit and oversized
sideburns was gone.

I took some of the money my mother left me to travel in
Ireland, although I felt like I shouldn't enjoy a trip so soon
after her death. So I didn't enjoy the Cliffs of Moher, the
music in Galway, or the golf with rented clubs in Kilkee.
The only part of the trip that really spoke to me was a drive
through the Burren—that desolate, rocky landscape in which
you expect to see a mad old Celtic monk tearing out his hair,
or Cú Chulainn constructing a dolmen for his dead son, or a
banshee flying over a stone fence.

I went there because mother's relatives emigrated from
Ireland, although the family history tying us to the old
country is lost. Once, I asked Mom if she had any pho-
tographs of her ancestors. Together, we pawed through a
cardboard box of faded pictures that had been in the back
of a closet since her own mother's death several years ago. In

a leather-covered album we found a tintype of a diminutive, carefully-dressed man standing on a footstool, his right hand tucked Napoleon-like in his vest. Below the picture in fading, spidery script was written, "The Family Dwarf, Killarney." At the cemetery, after a brief service in cold March sunshine, everyone hurried back to their cars. A few feet away from the grave, I turned back to take an extra rose from the bouquet that topped her casket and there he was, almost hidden among the rows of folding chairs. The Family Dwarf was more formal, somber, and grief-stricken than any of the mourners. He looked at me reproachfully with his zinc-colored eyes.

"Are you okay?" Paul asks. It's the same thing the undertaker had asked me as I stood on the artificial grass surrounding the grave. It takes me a moment to untangle myself from the memory, from the glare of the Family Dwarf who had disappeared when I turned back to him after assuring the undertaker I was alright.

"Sure," I say, "I'll be right back."

I walk unsteadily to the stall-sized bathroom where I wash my hands in the toy sink and splash what meager water I can coax out of the little faucet onto my face. Looking at myself in the smudged mirror for a moment I don't recognize myself. I look like someone who resembles me, but in a blurry, barely passable way.

When I return Paul has four more little bottles of brandy on the tray. "Different stewardess," he says, handing me two of them. As I pour the contents into my plastic glass Paul asks, "So what's your story?" Pitch me."

Again, it takes me a moment to understand that he wants me to tell him a story idea for his television show, and not get out a baseball and start playing catch in the aisle, or maybe

take him by his starched collar and calfskin belt and toss him
from the emergency exit out into the darkness. But then I do.
I tell him about Elvis and the dementia and the impersonator
and the morphine and the Family Dwarf. Partway through
my story he grabs his jacket, takes a silver pen out of a pocket, and starts scribbling notes on a couple of the insubstantial
airline napkins.

I fall asleep while he's telling me how excited he is about
my misfortune and wake up just as the pilot is telling us that
we are about to begin our descent. It's light outside the windows and Paul is shaving, using a tiny electric razor and the
mirror from a make-up compact. He looks disconcertingly
fresh and wide-awake.

We say good-bye in the terminal before heading off to
our connecting flights. I ask him if there's any chance I could
play myself. He shrugs. "Once people get the chance to see
how they look, most folks don't want to," he says. "We'll be
in touch." Part of me is sure he won't call, another is afraid
he will.

I watch him walk away until he is lost in the crowd of
people hurrying to their gates or trying to find the exit.

Unquestioned Forgiveness, Inc.

For penance I give LovingMom27 two hours of community service, since she's already picking up trash along the highway under court order. LovingMom27 is a chronic shoplifter. She has Unquestioned Forgiveness' Silver-level plan, which means, in addition to her chat room interactions with us, she can log in and have a Skype forgiveness session with a representative once a month—as she's doing now. Many of our customers with criminal convictions have been sentenced to community service, so I let that do double duty as penance. I figure their lives are tough enough as it is.

Under our corporate guidelines, I could simply tell my penitents to say a few Our Fathers and Hail Marys, repeat the Serenity Prayer X-number of times, or recite the company's own non-denominational, copyrighted Unquestioned Forgiveness Prayer:

> I am not a bad person,
> I only made a mistake.
> I am not a bad person,
> My life I will remake.

Customer reviews consistently show people like being given the Unquestioned Forgiveness Prayer to say, so corporate urges us to assign it. With that in mind I throw reciting the prayer in along with the community service for my chronic shoplifter. "Go in peace and forgiveness, Loving-Mom27," I say, and terminate our session.

We're required to say, "Go in peace and forgiveness," and end with the customer's user name. It always feels odd saying, "Go in peace and forgiveness, MeanBastard16," or,

"Go in peace and forgiveness, Hellbound82," but that's the policy. You never know when you're being monitored, so it's best not to deviate.

A username is required both for a customer's confidentiality and so the company doesn't get dragged into court. Most of the time customers ask to be forgiven for something like cheating—on taxes, on a final exam, or on a spouse. However, we get everything up to, and including, homicide. Corporate strongly suggests that Skype sessions be audio-only for penitents who have done something prosecutable—unless they've already been convicted—on the chance a Forgiver could be forced to testify.

That's my job title—Forgiver. Actually, Senior Forgiver. I've only been with Unquestioned Forgiveness for six months, but the company experiences a lot of turnover. Being a Forgiver can be stressful and it's a minimum wage job to start. The company tried to move some of its non-video Forgiving function to India but apparently customers, at least here in the U.S., don't want forgiveness from someone with an accent, or who sometimes uses non-standard sentence construction. I don't understand that. I mean, you two-time your spouse or, Christ, kill somebody, and you're upset the person offering you forgiveness speaks with a Punjabi lilt or gets an occasional colloquialism wrong? Because of that, only technical problems get transferred abroad.

Although the job isn't ideal, I enjoy working from home. Forgivers are required to dress professionally for video Skype sessions, but only for what appears on-screen. A lot of the time I pair my button-down shirt and knit tie with my favorite flannel pajama bottoms decorated with Day of the Dead skulls, and a pair of red plaid slippers.

In addition to the Skype and chat sessions, Forgivers

respond to text messages from customers with Bronze-level plans. Most of the replies boil down to, "Yes, you really are forgiven," or, "Yes, I am qualified to forgive you." Every Forgiver must be ordained. I, myself, am a minister in the Natural Earth Church based in Taos, New Mexico. I carry a card in my wallet that attests to my ordination, which cost $25. The company reimbursed me.

The Gold-level plan offers multiple monthly Skype sessions, and the Platinum-level plan features unlimited Skype sessions and twice-yearly in-person absolutions. The company has few of these higher-level subscribers. The bulk of our revenue comes from pay-as-you-go users who select their particular indiscretion from a "Forgive Me For..." pull-down menu. They then receive a pre-determined penance delivered with new age-y background music and a downloadable copy of the Unquestioned Forgiveness Prayer suitable for printing and framing. We accept all major credit cards, as well as PayPal.

I have my qualms about the job. We don't ask if customers are remorseful or not, or if they're really going to change their ways. That would negatively impact profits. On the other hand, if someone *is* remorseful shouldn't there be a path to forgiveness? On yet another hand I may simply be justifying my actions. I fear it's the latter.

I don't intend to do this forever. Although, if I stayed with the company, I could work my way up to management. But that would mean dealing with calls from customers angry at their already-light penance. And who needs that?

When I'm done being a Forgiver I'll use one of my complimentary log-ins to Unquestioned Forgiveness to be Forgiven for enabling through Forgiveness. That's not one of the options on the "Forgive Me For..." pull-down menu, but there is the generic, "What I've Done," selection. Analytics show "Forgive Me For What I've Done," is our customers' most popular choice. So at some point the company will forgive me for having been an employee, which seems only fair.

After all, I won't be forgiven for what I *didn't* do, the times I fell short by inaction. I would pay out-of-pocket for that, but corporate hasn't figured out how to monetize what never happened. However, Research and Development has its Regret Engineers working on the problem so there's likely to be a notice in the company newsletter soon, and a roll-out before a new offering of shares.

The Sorrow Vendor

Between when the Pope renounced his faith and the
Republic of Texas declared its independence, I ran the local
sorrow franchise. I used to spend a lot of time in bars during
those years trolling for customers. My drink of choice was a
Virgin Mary. I drank it to fit in but not lose my edge. Sometimes I'd give a little toast to the faithless Pope.

I, myself, never really understood the attraction. My
customers said that being on a sorrow binge wasn't itself so
much fun. But afterwards…ah, afterwards!

Most people recall those as dark years, but it was a good
time for me. I was my own boss, set my own hours and was
doing a steady business. Then I was arrested for selling to a
sorrow addict who was only supposed to get unhappiness,
and then only by prescription. It was a bogus charge.
My trial made some headlines and would have made more
if it hadn't coincided with statehood for Puerto Rico, which
happened soon after Texas seceded. People said the govern-
ment didn't want to lose a star on the flag—like a general
being demoted—plus the cost of removing, country-wide, all
those stars. D.C. was still screwed.

Then, soon after my acquittal, the Supreme Court ruled
that citizens have a constitutional right to as much sorrow
as they want. People were finally free to be connoisseurs of
sorrow. Collectors, aesthetes, and snobs of sorrow. Hoarders.
Gluttons.

I guess I could have started over. I still had my sample
case stocked with black ribbons and armbands, sunset post-
cards scrawled *glad you're not here*, reproductions of Gustave
Doré drawings, and pressed, desiccated roses. But by then
there was already all this foreign sorrow flooding the mar-

ket. Sudanese, Ethiopian, Yemeni—much heavier shit than anything I ever dealt. And cheap. I don't know how anyone makes a profit.

Now I'm living off my savings and my Social Security check, so I have to watch my pennies. But sometimes when it's happy hour and I'm feeling nostalgic, I'll swing by the Tiki Lounge for a drink. These days I have the bartender make mine bloody. I've earned it.

Objets du Désir

The man and his wife decide they will explore the little
tourist town separately during the afternoon and then meet
up for dinner. As he wanders around the warren of shops to
see if there are any worth visiting before hitting the beach,
he occasionally sees himself in the shop-front windows—
middle-aged and a little gray, but not balding. His reflection
reminds him to stand up straight to reduce his paunch. He is
about to head back to the motel and change into his swim-
ming trunks when he sees a store called "Objets du Désir."

Inside, the store has the requisite pressed-metal roof and
exposed brick walls. Sleek track fixtures provide soft light,
and classical music floats out from hidden speakers. The
inventory is what the man might find at any junk store—used
platform shoes, a tin dollhouse, obscure LPs—except this
place has only a few dozen items, each displayed carefully as
a work of art on highly polished wooden shelves. He checks
the price tag on a dented aluminum percolator-style coffee
pot. $500. Clearly, the place doesn't move much merchan-
dise, he thinks.

As he heads for the door, he notices a set of plastic
pastel party trays. They are kidney-shaped, and each has a
recessed circle in which sits a small bowl for chip dip. He is
flooded by the memory of his mother hosting a party and
setting out trays exactly like these loaded with potato chips,
and dip made from sour cream and dried onion soup mix. In
his mind's eye he sees his mother happier than he can ever
remember her—she who so often worried over the smallest
thing. They cost more than the coffee pot, and yet....

He can always put them back he thinks, trays in hand, as
he drifts toward the cash register. Then he sees the radio. It is

an old-school portable with multiple bands—AM, FM, short-
wave—a telescoping antenna, and knobs to adjust for treble
and bass. It is the same model his father won at a raffle and
listened to for years as he got ready for work in the pre-dawn
darkness. The chrome grille protecting the radio's speaker
is even scratched at one corner, just as he remembers. That
imperfection seems heartbreaking to him as he thinks about
the long hours his father put in as a foreman. He grabs the
radio.

They are supposed to be saving money for retirement.
They have even talked about taking their credit cards and
freezing them in a block of ice so they would have to be
thawed out for emergency use. He can see his card going into
the Frigidaire.

As he sets the trays and radio down on the counter,
he notices a miniature carpenter's bench next to the cash
register. He had one just like it, even down to its little saw
and hammer. He pushes it next to his other purchases and
hands his credit card to the attractive, bored looking cashier,
who has not offered to help him even though he is the only
customer. His total is almost a month's take-home pay. After
she returns the card and starts wrapping the trays in tissue
paper, he picks up the work bench and turns the handle, thin
as a toothpick, of its tiny vice.

"I saw this advertised in a comic book and begged my
parents to buy it for me," he tells the cashier. "I never built
stuff myself. Why did I want it so badly?"

The woman, who has placed the trays and radio in bags
emblazoned with the store's name, takes the toy from the
man and places it in a small cardboard box.

"Telling you that," she says quietly, "costs extra."

The Monty Hall Problem

Under certain circumstances, it is mathematically proven
you should change your mind. For example, say you're
young and have three boy and/or girlfriends you're juggling.
Your first choice is a sensitive philosophy major who, more-
over, has compelling blue eyes and with whom, you have
discovered, you are good in bed. At this point, you have a
one-in-three chance of making the right choice. However,
just then one of the other people you're juggling dumps
you, God knows why and good riddance. Now, by switching
your choice to the final candidate to whom you are, after
all, attracted, you double your chance of choosing the right
life partner to 66.6 percent repeating decimal, whereas if
you stick with the philosophy major your chances are still
33.3 repeating decimal percent. (Really. There have been
computer simulations of this.) For the equation to work you
must assume that this wrong choice was divulged not ran-
domly but revealed intentionally by karma or God or the
TV game show host Monty Hall. Karma or God or Monty
Hall aside, you decide to stay with the sensitive and sexually
compatible choice because you don't want to experience the
pang of having had a good thing slip away—the theme for
any number of classic rock songs. Hall, host of "Let's Make
a Deal," exploited the difference between this mathematically provable strategy of switching and the emotional desire
to avoid regret. In each episode's final segment, a contestant chose one of three doors: behind one was a fantastic
prize, behind a second an okay prize, and behind a third
a "zonk"—some white elephant. So, after selecting Door
Number One, say, the contestant then got to see the set of
patio furniture hidden behind Door Number Two—nice, but

clearly not a life-changing prize. At this point, the contestant should switch and choose Door Number Three, because of the 66.6 percent versus 33.3 repeating decimal point percent chance of winning the fantastic prize. Despite this, most of the time contestants stuck with their first choice, because how would you feel if a lifetime supply of happiness was behind Door Number One after all? Awful. Awful is how you would feel. The corollary to this paradox is that the chance of completely avoiding regret is exactly zero. However, understanding this requires reaching that stage of life when doors stop opening, and start to close.

Elegy for the Corded Phone

Every time she calls me, I'm in the cemetery. I don't know how she does this. I try varying the time of day—or night—that I take my walk and sometimes cut through the cemetery at the end of my stroll instead of the beginning, but it makes no difference. That's when she calls.

"Hi," I'll typically say.

"Hi," she'll typically say in return. "Where are you?"

"Near the Tomkins," I'll tell her.

"They're in the section overlooking the lake, aren't they?" she'll ask.

"Yes," I'll say.

"That's nice. How are they?" she'll ask.

"Still dead," I'll answer.

That's our cue to move on to other topics: *Where are we going to eat dinner? What movie do you want to go see? Can you believe what the Governor did? I saw the cutest cat video on You Tube. How about those Red Wings?* Today starts out no differently.

"Hi," I say.

"Hi," she says. "Where are you?"

"Near the DeGroots," I tell her.

"Where are they?" she asks.

"Near the Civil War monument," I say. This is one of my favorite parts of the cemetery. I love the larger-than-life-size soldier wearing a stone overcoat and holding a lichen-covered rifle.

"Oh," she says. That's all, just, "Oh." After a few seconds I say, "It's a family plot. They seem to have been hit hard by the Spanish Flu epidemic back in '17," I offer.

"Oh," she says again. I sit down on the cement steps leading up to the Civil War graves. On the base of the soldier's statue the word "Charity" is chiseled into the granite. "Fraternity" and "Loyalty" are on the adjoining sides of the square base. The side opposite "Charity" and facing away from the gravel path is blank.

"How come every time I call you, you're in the cemetery?" she asks.

"How come every time I'm in the cemetery you call?" I ask. Or maybe answer.

"I've been thinking," she begins. What she has been thinking is that I am not the best boyfriend she could have. I want to say that, for starters, I'm retired, ergo no longer a boy, ergo free to walk through the cemetery whenever I damn well feel like it, but I don't, especially since she has just noted I am not really in touch with my feelings, and why have that be the first feeling I admit to? Also, I am not very demonstrative, she informs me.

What I feel is that I am on the verge of crying. Not because her observations are hurtful—which they are—but because they're true.

"What was that? I think you're breaking up on me," I say, and disconnect the call. Then I power down the phone.

I turn to my old friends, the Nygrens, Bruce, and Laura, who died within a couple years of each other back in the mid-80s. "'Oops, I guess I did it again,'" I say, although I know they will miss the reference. Their answer is the same as always, *There's not that much time*, although my wireless company assures me, month after month, that I have many, many minutes to spare.

Debt Obligations

It took so little collateral—an electric guitar unplugged from dreams, a collection of vintage bottle caps, a bundle of love letters from the dead. We are bound together by regret or misfortune, depending on who you ask.

Most days we amuse ourselves playing games of twenty questions or trying to stump each other with movie trivia.

Victor likes to have one of us sit on his back while he does push-ups. I feel weightless as he goes up and down smoothly as an oil rig.

Rhonda hopes we stay together.

How could that happen, asks Carlos.

Brigit isn't sure, but thinks it has to do with hedging.

After that, I imagine us all planted in a long row at the far edge of a manicured back yard. We can see the great house's wide, well-appointed loggia and a fountain whose sculpted mermaids jet sprays of water that fall back down into a scalloped basin with the sound of distant, continuous applause.

I confess this to Andre who sighs that it might not be so bad, all things considered.

Is it animal, Beth asks?

Yes, I say.

Dissenting Opinion from the Committee
for the Beatitudes

It's too bad, I guess, that no one able to quote chapter and verse survived what happened. For example, is it, *In the beginning God created the heaven and the earth,* or *In the beginning was the word and the word was with God and the word was God.* Or both?

I miss the long genealogical passages, those who-be-gat-whom litanies. When I was in college, I accepted a tiny green bible from a middle-aged proselyte (what that little book would be worth now!) and smoked some fine Columbian while wondering how they knew all those different generations when I couldn't even remember the name of my great-grandfather.

The Psalms Committee is taking suggestions for metaphors. This week it's what a woman's flowing hair should be compared to—a herd of horses cresting a hill? A willow tree in bloom? Water rushing over stones? One faction thinks we need to know who the woman is, what she represents, before we can describe her. Another believes those questions will be revealed through the description.

So far, we have eight Commandments, two Miracles, and five Stations of the Cross. *Blessed are the Meek,* I remind people when arguments get heated.

Oh, no, the chairman says. *That has yet to be decided.*

Acknowledgments

My thanks to the editors of the following journals, both print and electronic, in which these pieces first appeared—sometimes in earlier versions:

100 Word Story: "Divorce Party"
About Place Journal: "The Adoration"
Cheat Pop: "Electives and Requisites"
Cloudbank: "Elegy for the Corded Phone"
Extract(s): "The Biennese," "What I'd Say to Aliens"
Iron Horse Literary Review: "Dissenting Opinion from the Committee for the Beatitudes," "The Sorrow Vendor"
Journal of Compressed Creative Arts: "The Umamist"
On the Town: "The Origin of Omniscient Man"
Paper Darts: "The Sad Decline of the Sideshow"
Paris Review: "The Dauphin"
Peninsula Pulse: "Sins of Contrition"
Passages North: "Debt Obligations," "Paradoxes of the Space-Time Continuum"
Sips Card: "The Valentine Offensive"
Third Coast: "The Museum of Tears"

"Objets du Désir" received the Stella Kupferberg Memorial Short Story Prize from the public radio program *Selected Shorts* and was performed at Symphony Space in New York by David Rakoff.

"The Dauphin" was broadcast on National Public Radio's program *Weekend Edition: All Things Considered* as a part of its Three-Minute Fiction series read by Susan Stamberg.

"Divorce Party" also appeared in the anthology, *Nothing Short of 100*.

This book is for Sue William Silverman.

Colophon

Cover design by Bryson Hile
Cover Image from Pexels.com

Cover and interior set in Baskerville.

Etchings Press

Etchings Press is a student-run publisher at the University of Indianapolis. Each year, student editors choose the Whirling Prize, a post-publication award, in the fall and coordinate a publication contest for one poetry chapbook, one prose chapbook, and one novella in the spring. For more information, please visit etchings.uindy.edu.

Previous winners and publications

Poetry
2019: *As Lovers Always Do* by Marne Wilson
2018: *In the Herald of Improbable Misfortunes*
      by Robert Campbell
2017: *Uncle Harold's Maxwell House Haggadah* by Danny Caine
2016: *Some Animals* by Kelli Allen
2015: *Velocity of Slugs* by Joey Connelly
2014: *Action at a Distance* by Christopher Petruccelli

Prose
2019: *Dissenting Opinion from the Committee for the Beatitudes*
      by Marc J. Sheehan (fiction)
2018: *The Forsaken* by Chad V. Broughman (fiction)
2017: *Unravelings* by Sarah Cheshire (memoir)
2016: *Pathetic* by Shannon McLeod (essays)
2015: *Ologies* by Chelsea Biondolillo (essays)
2014: *Static: Stories* by Frederick Pelzer (fiction)

Novella
2019: *Savonne, Not Vonny* by Robin Lee Lovelace
2018: *Edge of the Known Bus Line* by James R. Gapinski
2017: *The Denialist's Almanac of American Plague and Pestilence* by Christopher Mohar
2016: *Followers* by Adam Fleming Petty

Marc J. Sheehan is the author of two full-length poetry collections—*Greatest Hits* from New Issues Poetry and Prose Press, and *Vengeful Hymns* from Ashland Poetry Press, which won the Richard Snyder Memorial Prize. His third collection of poems, *Limits to the Salutary Effects of Upper Midwestern Melancholy*, won *Split Rock Review*'s inaugural chapbook award. He has published stories, poems, essays, and reviews in numerous literary magazines, including *Paris Review*, *Prairie Schooner*, and *Michigan Quarterly Review*. His fiction has been featured on National Public Radio's Three-Minute Fiction series as well as performed onstage at Symphony Space in New York as part of the program, *Selected Shorts*. He lives in Grand Haven, Michigan.

www.ingramcontent.com/pod-product-compliance
Lightning Source LLC
Chambersburg PA
CBHW071013120726
47910CB00004B/1505